Ocean Animals

Biome Beasts

Lisa Colozza Cocca

Rourke
Educational Media

A Division of
Carson
Dellosa
Education

rourkeeducationalmedia.com

Before Reading: *Building Background Knowledge and Vocabulary*

Building background knowledge can help children process new information and build upon what they already know. Before reading a book, it is important to tap into what children already know about the topic. This will help them develop their vocabulary and increase their reading comprehension.

Questions and Activities to Build Background Knowledge:

1. Look at the front cover of the book and read the title. What do you think this book will be about?
2. What do you already know about this topic?
3. Take a book walk and skim the pages. Look at the table of contents, photographs, captions, and bold words. Did these text features give you any information or predictions about what you will read in this book?

Vocabulary: *Vocabulary Is Key to Reading Comprehension*

Use the following directions to prompt a conversation about each word.

- Read the vocabulary words.
- What comes to mind when you see each word?
- What do you think each word means?

Vocabulary Words:
- adapted
- baleen
- current
- echolocation
- electrical
- esca
- herd
- sensory
- vertical

During Reading: *Reading for Meaning and Understanding*

To achieve deep comprehension of a book, children are encouraged to use close reading strategies. During reading, it is important to have children stop and make connections. These connections result in deeper analysis and understanding of a book.

Close Reading a Text

During reading, have children stop and talk about the following:

- Any confusing parts
- Any unknown words
- Text to text, text to self, text to world connections
- The main idea in each chapter or heading

Encourage children to use context clues to determine the meaning of any unknown words. These strategies will help children learn to analyze the text more thoroughly as they read.

When you are finished reading this book, turn to the next-to-last page for **Text-Dependent Questions** and an **Extension Activity**.

Table of Contents

Biomes

A biome is a large region of Earth with living things that have **adapted** to the conditions of that region.

Ocean biomes cover about 70 percent of Earth's surface. The salt water in these biomes is always moving. It can be warm, cold, or partly frozen.

Bering Sea

NORTH AMERICA

Atlantic Ocean

Pacific Ocean

Caribbean Sea

SOUTH AMERICA

Southern Ocean

The Atlantic, Pacific, Indian, Arctic, and Southern Oceans are ocean biomes. The Bering, Mediterranean, Caribbean, Arabian, and South China Seas are also ocean biomes. Some bays and gulfs are ocean biomes too.

Arctic Ocean

EUROPE

ASIA

Mediterranean Sea

AFRICA

Arabian Sea

South China Sea

Indian Ocean

AUSTRALIA

ANTARCTICA

Ocean biomes are divided into three **vertical** zones. The aphotic zone is the deepest part of the ocean. The water is cold and completely dark. It has few food sources. The bottom of an ocean has low areas and high areas. When the land is higher, the water is not deep enough to have an aphotic zone.

Ocean Light Zones

Euphotic Zone

Disphotic Zone

Aphotic Zone

The disphotic zone, or twilight zone, is the middle layer. It receives some sunlight.

The euphotic zone is the top 656 feet (200 meters) of water where sunlight goes through. Most of the plants and animals in oceans live in this zone.

Did You Know?

The plants and algae growing in ocean biomes provide most of Earth's oxygen.

The Aphotic Zone

Animals in the aphotic zone often have extra-large eyes. The vampire squid is only about 6 to 12 inches (15 to 30 centimeters) long, but it has the same size eyeballs as a large dog. It has lights on the tips of each arm. It uses the lights to communicate with other vampire squid.

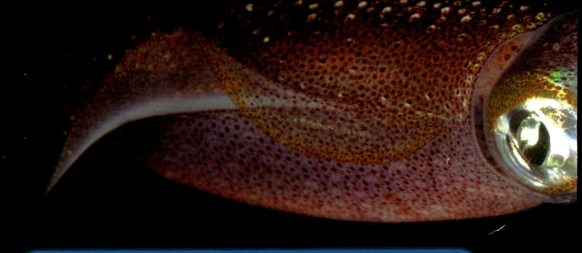

Did You Know?

Vampire squids eat marine snow, tiny bits of plants and animals that fall from the water above. The bits collect on sticky cells on their tentacles.

Like the vampire squid, the giant squid also lives in this zone. It has the largest eyes in the animal kingdom. Large eyes help these dark-dwellers absorb more light to spot prey and predators.

giant squid

esca

The anglerfish has a huge head with a large mouth. On females, a fin sticks out over the mouth. It looks like a fishing pole. A small organ, called an **esca**, sits at the tip of the pole. It holds millions of light-producing bacteria. The skin on the pole glows in the dark and draws other fish near.

The black swallower fish's long, hooked teeth close like a zipper. The fish follows prey and bites the tail. The teeth can be pushed inward to pull prey inside. Then the teeth are pushed forward to lock in the prey.

Did You Know?

Both the anglerfish and the black swallower fish can swallow prey twice their size. They are able to live for days on a single catch.

The Disphotic Zone

Most of the 300 kinds of octopuses live in the disphotic, or twilight zone. They can change colors to blend into their surroundings. Octopuses can also use their eight long arms to build dens with large rocks. They crawl inside and block the entrance with another rock to seal themselves off from predators.

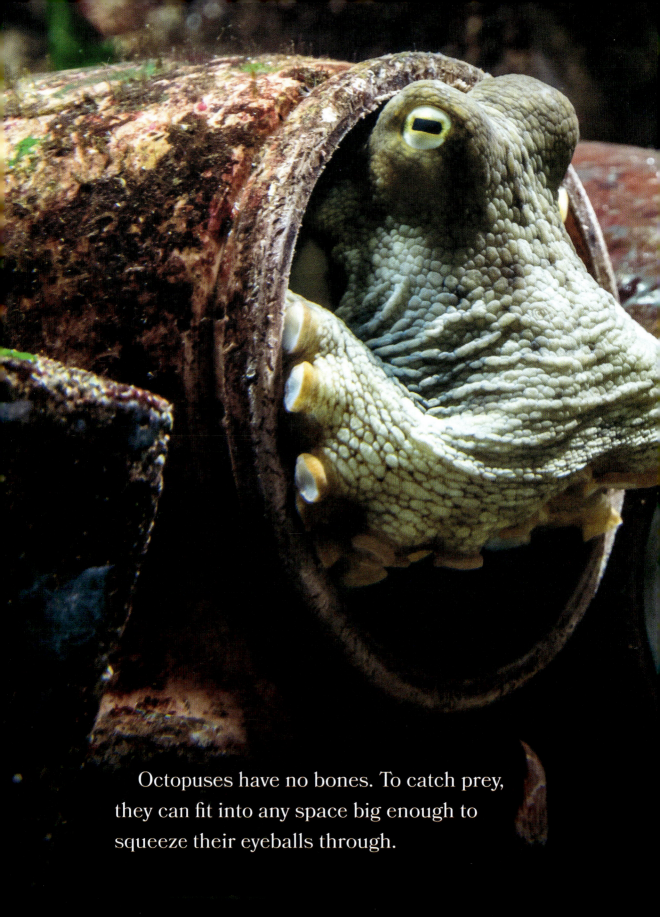

Octopuses have no bones. To catch prey,
they can fit into any space big enough to
squeeze their eyeballs through.

Snipe eels have long, thin bodies with threadlike tails. Their top jaw curves up and the lower jaw curves down. Their hooked teeth face backward. To catch prey, the eel opens its mouth and swishes its head back and forth. Shrimp get caught on the teeth and get pushed into the mouth.

Did You Know?

A person's spine has 33 bones. A snipe eel has 750 bones in its spine!

Jellyfish are not really fish. They have no spine. Their mouths are located inside their bell-shaped, bag-like bodies. Their tentacles have stinging cells.

Did You Know?

Jellyfish have been around for millions of years. They floated in oceans long before dinosaurs walked on Earth.

Jellyfish float with the **current** unless they are in danger. Then they shoot water from their mouths to move forward quickly. Jellyfish need less than a second to sting. The sting can stun or paralyze prey and predators.

The Euphotic Zone

The largest animal on Earth, the blue whale, lives in the euphotic zone. It can grow up to 100 feet (30.5 meters) long. Its tongue can weigh as much as an elephant. Its heart can weigh as much as a car.

Did You Know?

The blue whale eats more than four tons (3.6 metric tons) of krill each day.

The blue whale has grooves in the skin on its throat and chest that open like an accordion to take in water. Fringed plates of fingernail-like material, called **baleen**, hang from the upper jaw.

A blue whale gulps water, closes its mouth, then uses its tongue to push the water out through the baleen. The baleen catches small shrimp-like fish called krill so they can't escape with the water.

Bottlenose dolphins are among the smartest animals on Earth. They travel in groups called pods, and communicate with each other through squeaks and whistles.

Bottlenose dolphins will work as a group to **herd** fish together for an easy catch. They will even follow fishing boats and whales to eat their leftovers.

Did You Know?

Blue whales and bottlenose dolphins use **echolocation** to find prey. They make sounds underwater that bounce off prey and return. They listen for the echo to know where the prey is located.

Great hammerhead sharks have wide-set eyes that allow them to see prey swimming above, below, in front, and on either side of their heads. Special **sensory** organs spread over the head pick up **electrical** fields given off by other animals. The shark uses this information to find prey, such as stingrays, hiding under sand.

Seabirds

Many seabirds live in, around, and above the open ocean. The wandering albatross has the longest wingspan of any bird. It can glide for hours without flapping its wings.

The albatross can spot fish and squid in the water while soaring above the ocean. It swoops down and catches them with its long, hooked beak. Its excellent sense of smell helps it hunt in the dark. This bird eats garbage thrown from ships too.

The Atlantic puffin is sometimes called a sea parrot because of its colorful beak. This bird's small wings make taking flight difficult. It first scrambles across the water with its wings flapping very hard. Once it takes off, the bird can fly fast.

Did You Know?

The Atlantic puffin and the wandering albatross spend most of their life at sea. They only go ashore to breed and nest.

In water, the puffin's small wings work as flippers. The puffin uses them and its webbed feet to dive below the surface. Its waterproof feathers help it float on the water to rest.

The Atlantic puffin eats fish and eels. It collects prey one at a time until its beak is full. Its beak can hold about 20 fish! Then it eats the prey.

gentoo penguin

Did You Know?

Seventeen species of penguins live in ocean biomes. The round lenses in their eyes help them see underwater. Their ears adapt to the pressure of different depths of water as the penguins dive.

The ocean is Earth's largest ecosystem. It supports a variety of life, from the smallest fish to the largest mammal on Earth. And those are only the ones we know about. Many ocean species have yet to be discovered!

ACTIVITY: Blind Spot Experiment

Hammerhead sharks can spot prey in every direction. Most fish have one or more blind spots. People have blind spots too. Complete this experiment to better understand why the hammerhead's vision is important to its survival.

Supplies

- strip of blank white paper that measures about one inch by nine inches (2.5 by 23 centimeters)
- black marker

Directions

1. Draw a small black plus sign on one end of the paper strip and a small dot at the other end, leaving about a hand-length of white between them.
2. Hold the paper so the dot is to your left and the plus sign is to your right at an arm's length away.
3. Close your right eye and stare at the plus sign with your left eye.
4. Slowly move the strip closer as you stare at the plus sign. At what distance does the dot disappear from your view?
5. Repeat with your right eye open and your left eye closed.
6. Turn the paper so the plus sign is on top and repeat.
7. Flip the paper so the dot is on the top and repeat.
8. Try it with both eyes open.

The places where you could no longer see the dot are called blind spots. Why do you think having no blind spots helps the hammerhead shark?

Glossary

adapted (uh-DAPT-id): changed physical or social characteristics to suit a particular situation

baleen (buh-LEEN): fingernail-like material that hangs from the jaws of some whales

current (KUR-uhnt): the part of a body of water moving steadily in one direction

echolocation (ek-oh-loh-KAY-shuhn): process in which distant prey is located by sending out a sound and listening to the sound that bounces back off the prey

electrical (i-LEK-trik-uhl): containing currents or charges of electricity

esca (es-KUH): a light-producing organ found on some marine fish

herd (hurd): to move animals together into one place; dolphins herd fish by forming a circle around them and swimming inward to drive the fish toward the center of the circle

sensory (SEN-sur-ee): having to do with the senses: sight, hearing, taste, smell, or touch

vertical (VER-ti-kuhl): from top to bottom or bottom to top

Index

Text-Dependent Questions

1. What determines the different zones in the ocean?

2. What does the esca of an anglerfish hold?

3. What do jellyfish do to move quickly?

4. How do the grooves in the blue whale's throat and chest help it eat?

5. What do blue whales and dolphins use to find prey?

Extension Activity

Many ocean animals have sharp senses to help them survive in the ocean. If you could have a super-powered sense, which one would you choose? Why? How would it help you in your day-to-day life? Make a list of tasks you think would be easier to do with your super-powered sense.

About the Author

Lisa Colozza Cocca has enjoyed reading and learning new things for as long as she can remember. She lives in New Jersey by the coast and loves the feel of the sand between her toes. You can learn more about Lisa and her work at www.lisacolozzacocca.com.

www.rourkeeducationalmedia.com

PHOTO CREDITS: Cover and Title Page ©danilovi, ©wrangel, ©Louise Cunningham, ©Pobytov, ©Martin Prochazkacz; Pg 3, 8, 13, 18, 23 ©Pobytov; Pg 28, 30, 32 ©Global_Pics; Pg 4 ©CarlaNichiata; Pg 5 ©ttsz; Pg 6 ©Korovin; Pg 7 ©DeborahMaxemow; Pg 8 ©Konstantin Novikov; Pg 10 ©panparinda; Pg 12 ©Boban Vaiagich; Pg 14 ©Charles Lopez ; Pg 16 ©chonlasub woravichan; Pg 18 ©eco2drew; Pg 19 ©jocrebbin; Pg 20 ©Wild &Free; Pg 22 ©EXTREME-PHOTOGRAPHER; Pg 23 ©mauinow1; Pg 24 ©wildestanimal; Pg 25 ©mantaphoto; Pg 26 ©SoopySue; Pg 27 ©fieldwork; Pg 28 ©EXTREME-PHOTOGRAPHER

Edited by: Kim Thompson
Cover and interior design by: Kathy Walsh

Library of Congress PCN Data

Ocean Animals / Lisa Colozza Cocca
(Biome Beasts)
ISBN 978-1-73161-445-2 (hard cover)
ISBN 978-1-73161-240-3 (soft cover)
ISBN 978-1-73161-550-3 (e-Book)
ISBN 978-1-73161-655-5 (ePub)
Library of Congress Control Number: 2019932145

Rourke Educational Media
Printed in the United States of America,
North Mankato, Minnesota